Herself and Janet Reachfar

by Jane Duncan

Pictures by Mairi Hedderwick

This edition published in 2002 by
Birlinn Ltd, Edinburgh
Copyright © the Estate of
Jane Duncan 1975
Illustrations copyright ©
Mairi Hedderwick 1975
First published in 1975 by
MacMillan London Limited

ISBN 1 84158 209 3

Birlinn

EVERYBODY CALLED Janet "Janet Reachfar" because the farm which was her home was named "Reachfar". It lay on top of a hill in the Highlands of Scotland and looked down towards the sea.

The nearest house to Reachfar was two miles away but Janet never felt lonely. She had her dog called Fly and her

ferret called Angus. She also had her family: her grandfather
and grandmother, her father and mother, her aunt and her
special friends, Tom and George, who did most of the work
about the farm.

Janet's grandfather was very old, with a long white beard, and he was a little deaf. He spoke very seldom and went about the farm by himself. Janet saw her father only in the evenings, for he managed another farm all day. Her grandmother, her mother and Aunt Kate were usually too busy to talk to Janet very much – especially her grandmother, who, Janet thought, must be the busiest woman in the whole world.

Granny was always bustling about and "laying down the law" or being "on about" things, as George and Tom called it. Only they did not call her "Granny" when she was on about things – they called her "Herself".

One noonday in spring, when Janet and her family were sitting at the big kitchen table having their dinner, the sun

suddenly seemed to disappear and the sky went dark. Big flakes of snow began to fly past the window.

"I *told* you this was coming," Granny said, and it was in her "Herself" voice.

Granny always seemed to know when it was going to rain and when there was going to be a gale. George and Tom said that there was a little man who lived in the brown jug on the top shelf of the dresser who told Granny about the weather, but Janet knew that this was not true. One day, when everybody was out of the house, Janet had climbed right up and looked inside the jug and there was nothing in it but a few nails and a dead spider.

"I told you," Herself said again, "but none of you ever listens to *me*. *You* know best all the time."

This was not true either. Janet thought that everybody at Reachfar was always listening to Herself all the time. You could not help it.

"I said it was too early in the year to put the sheep out on the High Moor and the East Hill," Herself went on. "So don't blame me now that you have to go and bring them all back into the shelter of the Home Wood again."

She spoke as if everybody was arguing with her, but

nobody was saying a word. Everybody was watching the
snow, which was growing thicker and thicker and piling up
on the frames of the window-panes.

"*If Candlemas be bright and fair, half the winter's to
come and more*," Herself said. "And Candlemas this year
was like a day in June. So finish your dinner, George and
Tom, and fetch the sheep back into the wood."

"Yes, Mistress," Tom and George said together.

They put on their heavy coats and mufflers, took their tall sticks from the rack in the passage, and called their sheepdogs, Moss and Fan, out of the barn. Then they set off towards the gate that led to the High Moor. Janet followed them with Fly, but she did not go further than the gate. The High Moor was a forbidden place.

"We will gather the big flock off the Heights first, Tom," George said at the gate. "Those thirty ewes on the East Hill will have to wait till we get back. Run along into the house, Janet, out of all this snow and cold."

Janet and Fly turned back down the farmyard, but they did not go into the house. There was no point, with Herself on about nobody ever listening to her.

Janet went into the stable and climbed up to sit on the edge of Betsy's manger, while Fly lay down on a sack by the wall.

Stroking Betsy's face, Janet thought about her grandmother. She was a magic sort of person – something like a witch, but not an ugly or wicked witch. She was rather beautiful, really. Her "on-abouts" did not last for very long, and soon she would turn back into the person they called Granny, who was gentle and wise.

Almost magically wise, Granny always seemed to know where you had been and what you had been up to, even when you were far away out of her sight. It seemed to Janet that Granny knew not only about the weather, but about every single thing in the whole world.

Janet gave Betsy's neck a final pat and climbed down from the manger, saying inside her head the rhyme that she,

Tom and George had made:

> *When Herself is on-about*
> *The three of us are better out.*

Herself would have changed back into Granny by tea-time, but meanwhile Janet decided to go to the barn to have a chat with Angus, her ferret.

Angus, however, made it clear that he did not want to be chatted to. When Janet spoke to him, he opened his pink eyes for a moment, shut them again, snuffled, and curled himself up more tightly. Janet shut his box and went through the door at the end of the barn into the byre.

Maggie, the big black cow, was lying on her side in her stall among the warm straw. She was more welcoming. She gave her head a shake and her tail a twitch, inviting Janet and Fly to sit down and lean against her fat warm body. Then she went on chewing her cud, her big tongue flicking round and round inside her mouth.

Feeling the warmth of
Maggie, Janet began to think of the
poor sheep out on the cold East Hill.
She could not stop thinking about them. It
would take George and Tom a long time to bring
down the flock from the High Moor. The ewes on the East
Hill would have a very long wait . . .

Suddenly Janet stood up. She buttoned up her coat and
put on her woollen hood and gloves. "Heel, Fly," she said as
they left the warm steamy byre for the snow and cold out-of-
doors.

The East Hill was a long way off, and today it seemed
longer than ever. The wind kept trying to blow Janet and Fly
backwards as they plodded through the deepening snow on
the path through the wood. At last, though, they came to the
little gate that led out of the corner of the wood onto the
bare hill where the snow was like a thick cloud of feathers.

When Janet took off her glove to undo the latch of the
gate, her fingers went stiff with the cold. The East Hill was a
forbidden place, too – but Janet did not intend to go right
out onto it, not *right* out *on* to it.

"Seek, Fly!" she said, waving her arm at the hill just like
Tom or George. "Sheep! Go seek!"

The dog crouched low, so that her dark furry body seemed to slide under the blowing snow. She ran out onto the hill, while Janet waited in the shelter of the trees by the gate.

Soon the sheep began to come towards Janet. "One, two, three –" she counted as the woolly creatures galloped one by one through the narrow gateway, baa-ing as if to say thank you for the shelter of the trees.

"Twenty-nine," Janet said when Fly came to look up at her. "One more, Fly! Go seek!"

Fly disappeared into the snow again and was gone for a long time. When she came back she brought no sheep with her.

She put her paws up to Janet's chest and then began to dance round and round, barking all the time and making bigger and bigger circles that took her further and further out on the hill.

She wanted Janet to follow her, but Janet was not sure about this. Besides being forbidden, the East Hill under the blowing snow was very wild, bare and frightening. In the end, though, she decided to trust Fly, who always knew the way home. She shut the little gate and stepped out into the deep snow and driving wind.

She was completely out of breath and her legs felt as if they were going to break with tiredness when, at last, Fly nuzzled into a hummock of snow and exposed the head of a sheep.

"Baa-aa," the sheep said in a weak tired voice as Janet and Fly began to dig the snow away. Fly dug very quickly with her fore-paws, making the snow fly up in a cloud behind her. But it was Janet who found the baby lamb, quite newly born and tucked in close to its mother.

"Stop, Fly," Janet said, for she knew that if she picked up the lamb and began to walk away, the mother sheep would struggle free and follow her.

Janet unbuttoned her coat, put the lamb inside, and fastened the coat again with the lamb's head sticking out between the two top buttons. When Janet and Fly started to walk away, the mother

sheep began to struggle
hard, baa-ing pitifully. It seemed
she could not get up.

"Dig, Fly!" Janet said, and soon they
found that a piece of the wire fence was wound
round and round the sheep's leg. Her struggling was only
pulling it tighter, so that it was cutting the leg painfully.

Janet's hands were not strong enough to bend the wire,
though she tried for some time. At last she sat down in the
snow, her chin resting on the lamb's head, which stuck out
on her chest. Fly sat down too, her head on one side, her
golden eyes looking from the sheep to Janet as if to say,
"What do we do now?"

This was the first time, Janet thought, that Fly had ever
asked her this question. Until now Fly had always known
best what to do. Fly knew that the stackyard ladder was too
high to climb and took Janet's skirt in her sharp teeth and
pulled her down. Fly knew that the ice on the duckpond
was not thick enough to walk on and pulled Janet back.
But now it was up to Janet.

She thought hard. Then she took off her
woollen hood and untied her blue hair-ribbon.
Her fingers were numb as she tied the ribbon
tightly to Fly's collar. Her lips were stiff
with cold too, as she said, "George
and Tom, Fly! George and Tom!"

Fly did not want to go. She
turned her head to sniff at the
ends of ribbon, then looked
back at Janet.

"Fetch, George, Tom!" Janet repeated sternly, pointing across the hill to where she thought the wood and home were. She could not be sure. The flying snow made the air so blackly dark that it seemed to shut all the world away.

Suddenly Fly made up her mind. With the wind behind her now, she dashed away, the ends of the blue ribbon streaming from her collar.

Janet tucked herself close into the woolly side of the sheep, took off her wet gloves, and put her cold hands inside her coat to cuddle the lamb. She tried not to feel frightened.

The snow piled up around them, while the wind howled and shrieked across the hill. Janet began to feel warm, cosy and sleepy, as if the world and the storm were going further and further away. She did not know that this deceiving warm sleepiness sometimes causes people to snuggle down and be found long afterwards, frozen to death.

She was quite startled when she heard barking close beside her. Fly began to dig, her blue ribbon still streaming in the wind, and then Moss and Fan were there and began to dig too.

"Out of it! Get back, dogs!" said George's voice, and Janet found herself being lifted, shivering now, out of the snowy hole that had been so cosy and warm.

George turned her over his arm and began to pat her quite hard on the back. The shivering stopped.

"Careful!" she said, coming wide awake. "Mind my lamb, you clumsy big lump!"

"Merciful goodness," Tom said. "She has a lamb!"

"The mother sheep is hurt," Janet told them. "She has got wire –"

"We'll soon see to that," Tom said, and with his strong fingers he began to untwist the wire that Janet had not been able to bend.

Janet was safe now from the storm, standing beside George and Tom, who always made everything safe. But she began to feel another kind of fear. She suddenly remembered that she was forbidden to come out onto the East Hill like this, and that there would be a scolding from Herself when she got home.

With the lamb's head still under her chin, Janet looked up at George. "Herself and Mother are going to be angry," she said.

"Angry? After you bringing in the flock from the Hill and bringing home the first lamb of the spring?" George asked. "Have you gone foolish in your head?"

The mother sheep gave a loud "Baa!" and sprang to her feet. She was limping a little, but she would soon be all right. She came close to Janet to sniff at her lamb's head.

"About the East Hill, here," Janet said, "Herself will be very angry."

"*What* East Hill?" George asked, looking around as if he had never heard of the East Hill. "Speaking for myself, I cannot see anything through all this snow. I do not see any East Hill around here."

"Nor me either, forbye," Tom said. "And besides, it is my opinion that we are no further from home than the fence around the wood. And I will tell you something more. We are going to be late for tea, and Herself will be so angry about that, likely she will have no angriness left for anything else. Come on!"

They all began to walk with the snow
blowing behind them. Janet had no idea of the
way home but that did not matter, for not only was Fly
there but George and Tom as well.

As they walked, they began to make a rhyme, and by the
time they reached the gate into the farmyard it was finished.
They told it to Herself as soon as they went into the house:

Janet found the first-born lamb
Near the East Hill gate.
Its mother's leg was stuck in some wire
And that is why we are late.

Herself looked from Tom to George, and then on to Janet with the lamb's head under her chin. This was her suspecting look – the look she wore when she suspected that Janet, George and Tom had been up to something.

"Baa!" the little lamb said in a small voice.

"That is enough of your silly rhymes and nonsense," Herself said sternly. "George, take that lamb out to the fold to its mother where it belongs."

"Right away, Granny," George said, beginning to undo Janet's coat.

"This very minute, Granny," Tom said.

Now Janet knew that everything was all right. But she also knew that on their way to the fold with the lamb, George and Tom would be calling Granny "Herself", for she was still laying down the law.

"And you take those wet things off," she was saying to Janet, "and sit down at the table beside *your* mother where *you* belong."

Janet did as she was told and Herself went on, "Sometimes I think the people of Reachfar have no sense at all, putting sheep out, taking them in, and prowling about among the snow and the cold as if they had no brains in their heads. It is a wonder that some of them don't get lost in the snow."

Janet's mother was very quiet and spoke always in a soft voice. She spoke now. "If they got lost in the snow, Granny, you would have nobody to scold. That would be terrible, wouldn't it?" she said.

Herself looked at Mother, and Janet watched her change back into Granny. Mother could always make her do this.

Granny smiled at Janet. "But you are a clever girl, finding the first lamb of the spring like that," she said. "Eat a big tea. You must be very hungry after going such a long, *long* way, all by yourself, to find that lamb."

Granny took the lid off the big black pot on the fire and stirred the supper soup. With the firelight shining on her face and white hair, she did look like a witch – a wise, kind sort of witch, who knew by magic that you had gone to a forbidden place, but that you had done it for a good reason and must be forgiven.

Janet Reachfar ate a boiled egg, a scone with butter, two scones with raspberry jam and a piece of shortbread. It was a very satisfactory tea.